cl🍀verleaf books™

Off to School

11.50

D1239593

Michael Makes Friends at School

Martha E. H. Rustad

illustrated by Paula J. Becker

Ⓜ MILLBROOK PRESS • MINNEAPOLIS

For Heather —MEHR

Millbrook Press
A division of Lerner Publishing Group, Inc.
241 First Avenue North
Minneapolis, MN 55401 USA

For reading levels and more information, look up this title at
www.lernerbooks.com.

Main body text set in Slappy Inline 22/28.
Typeface provided by T26.

Library of Congress Cataloging-in-Publication Data

Names: Rustad, Martha E. H. (Martha Elizabeth Hillman), 1975–
    author. | Becker, Paula, 1958– illustrator.
Title: Michael makes friends at school / by Martha E.H. Rustad ;
    illustrated by Paula J. Becker.
Description: Minneapolis : Millbrook Press, [2018] | Series:
    Cloverleaf Books—Off to School | Includes bibliographical
    references and index. | Audience: Ages: 5–8. | Audience:
    Grades: K to Grade 3. | Description based on print version
    record and CIP data provided by publisher; resource not
    viewed.
Identifiers: LCCN 2016043765 (print) | LCCN 2017011517
    (ebook) | ISBN 9781512451061 (eb pdf) | ISBN 9781512439373
    (library binding : alk. paper) | ISBN 9781512455779 (paperback
    : alk. paper)
Subjects: LCSH: Schools—Juvenile literature. | Friendship in
    children—Juvenile literature.
Classification: LCC LB1556 (ebook) | LCC LB1556 .R87 2017
    (print) | DDC 371—dc23

LC record available at https://lccn.loc.gov/2016043765

Manufactured in the United States of America
1-42150-25423-3/22/2017

TABLE OF CONTENTS

First Day!

Today is my first day at a new school. I'm a little nervous about meeting the other kids in my class.

But my mom tells me that the other kids can be my new friends!

Mom says that a friend is someone you like to be with.

It's fun to talk to and laugh with friends. But to make a friend, you have to be a friend too.

Friends care for one another. They want one another to be happy and safe.

I decide to look for kids who look like they might need a friend.

Chapter Two
Classroom Buddies

When I find my classroom, my teacher says, "Welcome, Michael! I'm Mrs. Robertson."

She says I can sit on the rug and look at a book with the other kids in my class.

I sit next to another boy.

"I'm Bradley," he says. "What's your name?"

"Michael," I tell him.

Then two girls come over.

"Hi! I'm Ava, and she's Willa," one girl says.

We show each other the books we are reading. Willa and I both like books about animals.

Friends share books, toys, and ideas with one another.

"Hello, class," Mrs. Robertson says. "Let's talk about friendship today."

We make a list of how to be friends in the classroom.

"Be kind," says Willa.

I say, "Include everyone."

"Help each other learn," says Bradley.

Chapter Three

Lunchroom Pals

At lunchtime, we go to the lunchroom.
I wonder where I will sit.

One boy sits all alone, so I go to his table.

"I'm Michael," I tell him.

He says, "I'm Seth. Do you want to sit by me?"

Seth and I talk while we eat lunch.
We find out that we both like to play soccer.
He has a dog, and I have a cat.
We like today's lunch.

"I could eat three hamburgers," I say.
"I could eat ten!" he jokes.

Friends don't always like all the same things. Good friends listen to one another and respect one another's differences.

Chapter Four

Playground Friends

At recess I see all my new friends!

19

When the day is done, I say good-bye to my teacher.
I tell my new friends, "See you tomorrow!"

Make a Friendship Band

Friendship bands are made of string. Use a cardboard circle to weave a simple pattern and make a band for a friend.

What You Will Need

a round cup

thin cardboard, such as an old cereal box

a pencil

a scissors

an adult to help

seven pieces of string or yarn, each about 18 inches (46 centimeters) long

What You Do

1) Place the cup upside down on the cardboard. Outline the cup to trace a circle.

2) Cut out the circle. Mark eight lines around the circle and a dot in the middle. The lines should be about 0.5 inches (1 cm) long.

3) Cut on the lines to make eight slots. Ask an adult to help you poke a sharp pencil through the middle dot to make a hole.

4) Gather the seven strings together. Tie a knot in one end.

5) Push the knot through the center of the circle. Place one string in each slot. One slot will not have a string in it.

6) Count three strings over from the open slot. Pull that string out of its slot, and move it into the open slot.

7) Repeat the pattern. Every once in a while, pull gently on the knot. You will see a band form.

8) Stop when the band is long enough to go around your wrist. Remove the strings from the slots. Tie a knot in the end. Give the friendship band to a friend.

GLOSSARY

decide: to make a choice

friend: a person who likes and trusts another person

friendship: being friends with another person

include: to make a part of

nervous: a feeling of worry or unease

recess: a break during the school day

BOOKS

Austen, Mary. *I Learn from My Friends.* New York: PowerKids, 2017. Read about sharing and playing with friends.

Orr, Tamra B. *Friendliness.* Ann Arbor, MI: Cherry Lake, 2017. Learn more about meeting neighbors and making new friends.

Plattner, Josh. *Manners with Friends.* Minneapolis: Abdo, 2016. Find out how to show good manners around friends.

WEBSITES

Friendship
http://www.cyh.com/HealthTopics/HealthTopicDetailsKids
.aspx?p=335&np=286&id=1636
Read more about what you can do to be someone's friend.

How Cliques Make Kids Feel Left Out
http://kidshealth.org/en/kids/clique.html
Learn what a clique is and how to be a better friend.

LERNER ℮ SOURCE™
Expand learning beyond the printed book. Download free, complementary educational resources for this book from our website, www.lerneresource.com.